Big and Little Stories

By MICHAELA MUNTEAN
Illustrated by MAGGIE SWANSON

Featuring Jim Henson's Sesame Street Muppets

A GOLDEN BOOK • NEW YORK
Western Publishing Company, Inc.
Racine, Wisconsin 53404

Q R S T

Big Bird's Big Story

Hello, everybody! I am here
to give you a tour of Sesame Stree
and to introduce you to some
of my friends. This is Oscar.
He likes big messes.

Now I'd like you to meet my friend
Mr. Snuffle-upagus. He likes big bowls
of spaghetti.

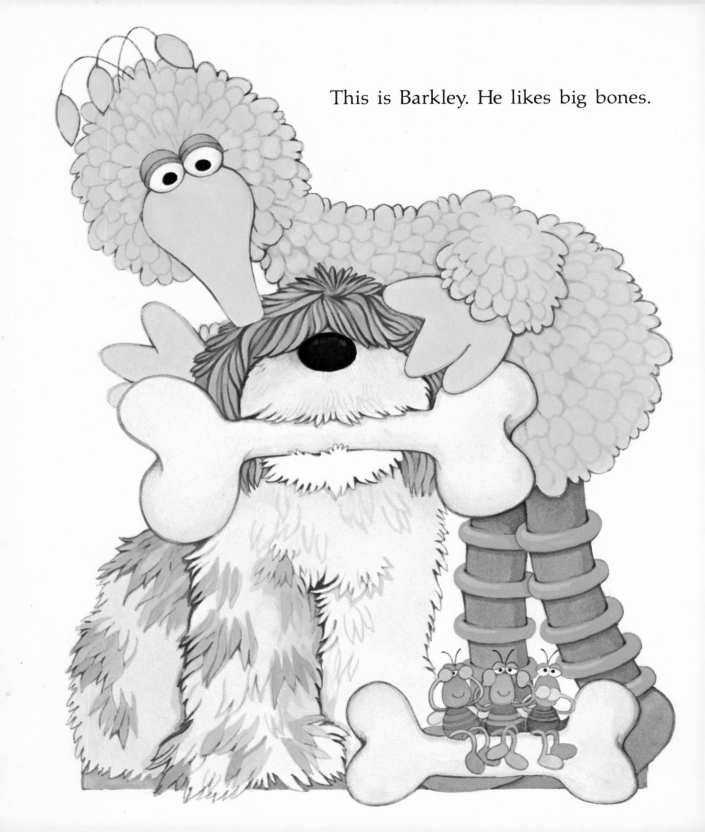

This is Barkley. He likes big bones.

This is Cookie Monster. He likes big cookies, but watch out for flying crumbs!

And I am Big Bird. I like big bags of bird seed,
a big nest to curl up in . . .

. . . and big hugs from my Granny Bird!

The Birthday Cake

Tomorrow is Bert's birthday. I will make him a little cake in this little pan. I will ask Little Bird to come to a little birthday party for Bert.

But if I make a *bigger* cake in this *bigger* pan, I can ask Little Bird and Big Bird to come to a bigger birthday party for Bert.

But if I use the *biggest* pan we have, I can make the *biggest* cake ever and ask everyone to come to the biggest party Sesame Street has ever had!

Gee, Bert is in for a big surprise!

The Amazing Mumford and his Magic Balloon Act

This is a little balloon. Soon it will be a *big* balloon.

A LA PEANUT BUTTER SANDWICHES!!!

Now this is a big balloon, but soon it will be a *bigger* balloon.

Hmmm...
The Amazing Mumford
and his assistant
have just made this
balloon disappear!

Big and Small Story

Herry Monster's coat is too small.
Bert's coat is too big.
Betty Lou's coat is just right.

Now Herry's coat is just right.
But Bert's coat is too small.
And Betty Lou's coat is too big.

At last everyone's coat is just the right size.

But what about the hats?

Little By Little

Little by little,
I'm getting bigger.
I grow every day. I can
reach the kitchen counter.

I can sit at the table
without a telephone book
to make me taller.

I can get my own cup
of water when I wake up.

I can swing
without getting
a push.

Little by little, I'm getting bigger!

Betty Lou's Twiddlebug Story

If I were a Twiddlebug,
I'd live in a little house.

I would wear little
Twiddlebug clothes.

I'd play with little twiddle toys.

I'd sleep in a little Twiddlebug bed.

And I would twiddle a happy little twiddle tune all night long.